EARLIER AMERICAN MUSIC
EDITED BY H. WILEY HITCHCOCK
for the *Music Library Association*

13

THE SOCIAL ORCHESTRA

STEPHEN FOSTER

THE SOCIAL ORCHESTRA

For Flute or Violin

*A Collection of Popular Melodies Arranged as
Solos, Duets, Trios, and Quartets*

NEW INTRODUCTION BY H. WILEY HITCHCOCK
*Director, Institute for Studies in American Music,
Brooklyn College, CUNY*

DA CAPO PRESS • NEW YORK • 1973

This Da Capo Press edition of
The Social Orchestra is an unabridged
republication of the first edition published
in New York in 1854.

Library of Congress Catalog Card Number 79-169645
ISBN 0-306-77313-9

Copyright © 1973 by the Music Library Association

Published by Da Capo Press, Inc.
A Subsidiary of Plenum Publishing Corporation
227 West 17th Street, New York, New York 10011

EDITOR'S FOREWORD

American musical culture, from Colonial and Federal Era days on, has been reflected in an astonishing production of printed music of all kinds: by 1820, for instance, more than fifteen thousand musical publications had issued from American presses. Fads, fashions, and tastes have changed so rapidly in our history, however, that comparatively little earlier American music has remained in print. On the other hand, the past few decades have seen an explosion of interest in earlier American culture, including earlier American music. College and university courses in American civilization and American music have proliferated; recording companies have found a surprising response to earlier American composers and their music; a wave of interest in folk and popular music of past eras has opened up byways of musical experience unimagined only a short time ago.

It seems an opportune moment, therefore, to make available for study and enjoyment—and as an aid to furthering performance of earlier American music—works of significance that exist today only in a few scattered copies of publications long out of print, and works that may be well known only in later editions or arrangements having little relationship to the original compositions.

Earlier American Music is planned around several types of musical scores to be reprinted from early editions of the eighteenth, nineteenth, and early twentieth centuries. The categories are as follows:

Songs and other solo vocal music
Choral music and part-songs
Solo keyboard music
Chamber music
Orchestral music and concertos
Dance music and marches for band
Theater music

The idea of *Earlier American Music* originated in a paper read before the Music Library Association in February, 1968, and published under the title "A Monumenta Americana?" in the Association's journal, *Notes* (September, 1968). It seems most appropriate, therefore, for the Music Library Association to sponsor this series. We hope *Earlier American Music* will stimulate further study and performance of musical Americana.

H. Wiley Hitchcock

INTRODUCTION

In the spring of 1853, at the peak of his career as America's most successful songwriter, Stephen Foster signed an exclusive contract with the New York music publishers Firth, Pond & Company. Soon thereafter, probably with the aim of tapping a new market for his music, he set about compiling an anthology of instrumental music, including in it a number of his own works, some arranged from songs but others originally conceived as instrumental pieces. *The Social Orchestra,* as the anthology was called, came out early in 1854 and sold for one dollar a copy. Foster was paid a flat one hundred and fifty dollars for his work; he must later have regretted the lack of provision for royalties, since the volume was a considerable success—indeed, past his death in 1864 and into the late 1880's.

The Social Orchestra can be viewed in several ways. It is, first of all, a collection of songs, dances, and opera airs popular among genteel music-lovers in pre-Civil War America; as such, it is a revealing historical document of the taste of the time. Second, it contains all but a handful of Foster's instrumental works, thereby extending our usual (and generally correct) view of him as primarily a songwriter. Third, as intended, it was, and remains viable as, a reservoir of pieces for amateur chamber music-making—"suitable," as the editors remark, "for serenades, evenings at home, etc." *The Social Orchestra* is not, and should not be viewed as, concert music of any pretensions whatsoever. It is frankly and modestly "household music," music to play more than to listen to, as insubstantial and entertaining as soap bubbles and as mid-nineteenth-century American as pumpkin pie. The printed music itself, especially the dances (and the book is full of Civil War-era favorites—waltzes, schottisches, quadrilles, polkas, redowas, jigs, and marches), is clearly skeletal, to be fleshed out in performance by whatever instruments (or musical impulses) are at hand: witness Foster's somewhat awkward "second violin" parts in the trio and quartet pieces; in double-stops throughout, they are obviously written so as to make them transferable to a pianist's right hand if only one fiddler is available.

A glance through the volume reveals the composers mid-nineteenth-century America was aware of and looked up to. Most are European: the aim of the book, as the *Musical World* remarked in reviewing it (February 25, 1854), was to "improve the taste of the community for social music," and the general view was that European music was more "tasteful" than American. Donizetti, Bellini, Mozart, Boieldieu, and Weber figure importantly. Already by 1854 Schubert's *Serenade* was not to be omitted from such an anthology. Two waltzes by Lanner are included, one of which, otherwise forgettable, was to be immortalized later by Stravinsky, who borrowed it for use in *Petrushka.*

More interesting from our standpoint are the instrumental works that Foster himself contributed. Apart from the melodies of well-known songs which he gives in instrumental solo and duet versions, the following are especially notable:

Anadolia (solo for flute or violin): who would have imagined from Foster such a cross between a Bellini aria and *Old Folks at Home?*

Jennie's Own Schottisch (trio): a simple but strong dance piece.

Village Festival (quartet): four quadrilles and a jig, with dance instructions like "Right & Left," "Forward Two," etc.

Old Folks Quadrilles (quartet): beginning with a quadrille fashioned from *Old Folks at Home* (which suggests how completely we have sentimentalized, and weakened, this essentially straightforward, square-cut tune), this continues with quadrille versions of *Oh, Boys, Carry Me 'Long, Nelly Bly,* and *Farewell, My Lilly Dear;* it ends with *Plantation Jig,* published earlier for piano solo as *Cane Brake Jig.*

H.W.H.

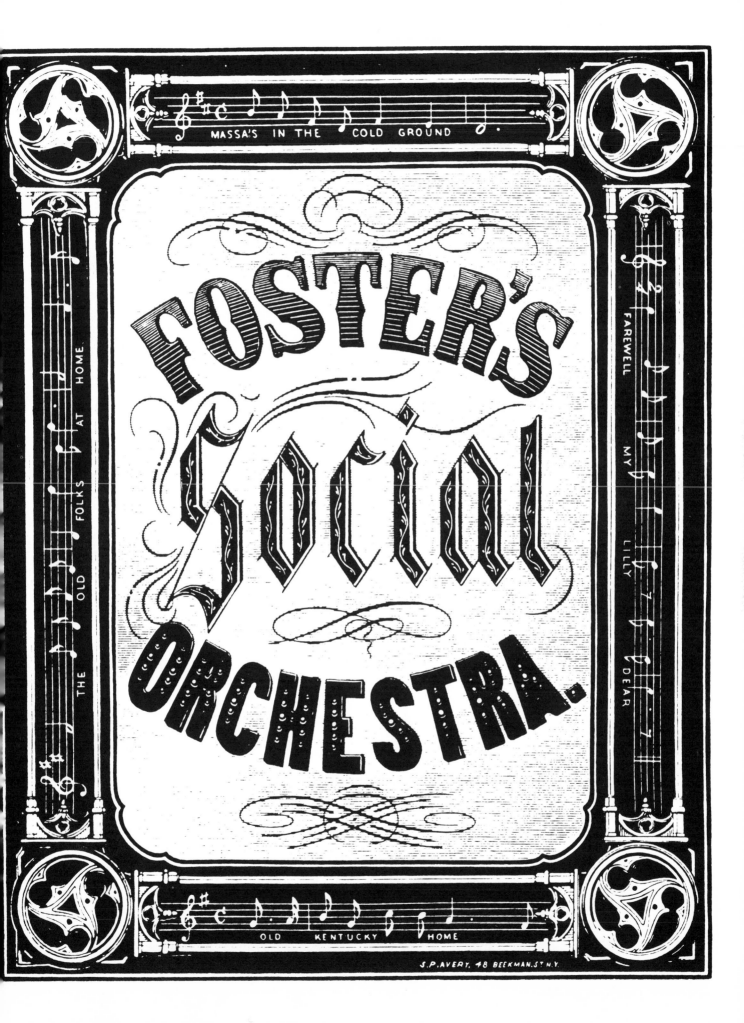

THE

SOCIAL ORCHESTRA

For Flute or Violin:

A COLLECTION OF POPULAR MELODIES

ARRANGED AS

SOLOS, DUETS, TRIOS, AND QUARTETS.

By STEPHEN C. FOSTER,
AUTHOR OF "NELLY BLY," "OLD DOG TRAY," ETC.

New York:
PUBLISHED BY FIRTH, POND & CO.,
No. 1 FRANKLIN SQUARE.
BUFFALO: J. SAGE & SONS. ST. LOUIS: WAKELAM & IUCHO.
DETROIT: A. COUSE.
1854.

INTRODUCTION.

THE publishers herewith offer to the public a collection of INSTRUMENTAL MUSIC, the melodies of which have been taken from among the most popular operatic and other music of the day, and arranged in an easy and correct manner, as Solos, Duetts, Trios, and Quartets, suitable for serenades, evenings at home, &c. Having long noticed the want of such a work, they have determined to issue one that will meet with general approbation, and have accordingly confided the task of selecting and arranging the melodies to a gentleman of acknowledged musical taste, and composer of some of the most popular airs ever written in this or any other country, as will be seen by reference to the name on the title page.

In the Trios and Quartets the Bass part is primarily intended for the Violoncello, though in its absence any other Bass instrument may be used, in many of the pieces, with the proper transpositions, and where both the Bass and second Violin are wanting, the parts written for them can be performed on the Piano-Forte, with good effect.

NEW YORK, January, 1854.

CONTENTS.

PART I. SOLOS.

PART II. MELODIES ARRANGED AS DUETS.

PART III. MELODIES ARRANGED AS TRIOS.

PART IV. MELODIES ARRANGED AS QUARTETS.

THE
SOCIAL ORCHESTRA.

PART FIRST.

OLD DOG TRAY.

S. C. FOSTER.

TWILIGHT SONG.

H. W. POND.

I LOVE THE MERRY SUNSHINE.

S. GLOVER.

OLD FOLKS AT HOME.---With Variations.

E. P. CHRISTY.

WILL YOU COME TO MY MOUNTAIN HOME.

F. H. BROWN.

HOHNSTOCK POLKA.

6

SARATOGA LAKE WALTZ.

LOVE LAUNCHED A FAIRY BOAT.

TULLY.

WIDOW MACHREE.

S. LOVER.

WALTZ BY BEETHOVEN.

Con espressione.

Dolce.

COMMENCE YE DARKEYS ALL.

W. D. CORRISTER.

BRIDAL WALTZ.

JULLIEN.

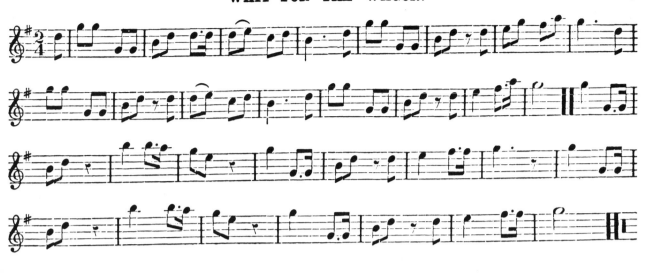

NANCY TILL.

CALLY POLKA.

O WOULD I WERE A BOY AGAIN.

F. ROMER.

NELLY WAS A LADY.

S. C. FOSTER.

SONTAG POLKA.

D'ALBERT.

EULALIE.

Poco Lento.   S. C. FOSTER.   **11**

ROLL ON, SILVER MOON.

SLOMAN.

Andante.

MY OLD KENTUCKY HOME, GOOD NIGHT.

S. C. FOSTER.

Moderato.

12

THOU ART GONE FROM MY GAZE.

G. LINLEY.

ON THE BANKS OF GUADALQUIVER.

LAVENU.

I'D OFFER THEE THIS HAND OF MINE.

L. T. CHADWICK.

THE WILD HAUNTS FOR ME.

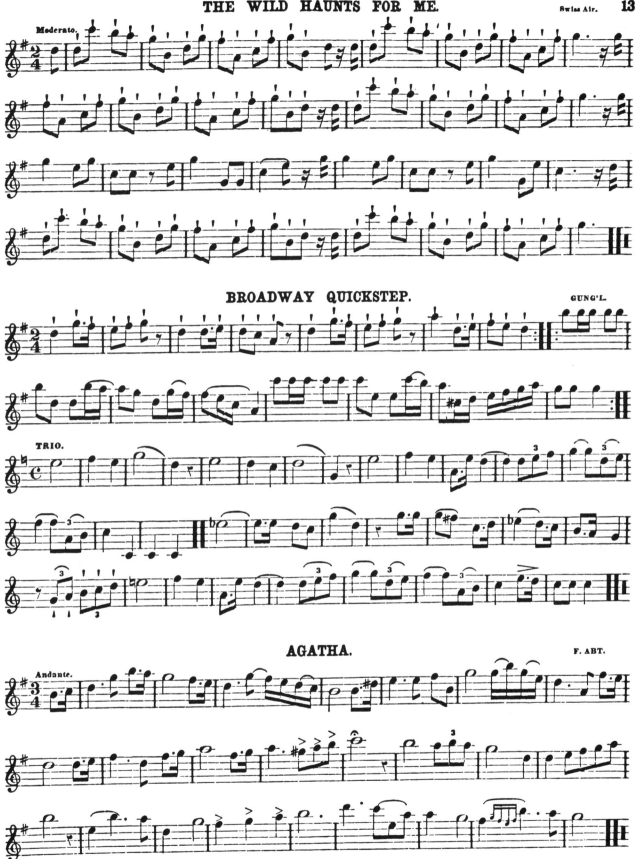

BROADWAY QUICKSTEP.

GUNG'L.

TRIO.

AGATHA.

F. ABT.

EVENING STAR WALTZ.

LANNER.

PEARL POLKA.

H. KLEBER.

SCENES THAT ARE BRIGHTEST.

W. V. WALLACE.

COME WHERE THE FOUNTAINS PLAY

DONIZETTI.

WILL YOU LOVE ME THEN, AS NOW?

IRENE.

S. C. FOSTER.

ITALIAN MELODIES. No. 2.

DONIZETTI.

Allegretto quasi Andante.

MOZART.

Andante.

ANADOLIA.

Andante Cantabile.

S. C. FOSTER.

PART SECOND.

Melodies Arranged as Duetts.

DUETT FROM LUCIA DI LAMMERMOOR.

DONIZETTI.

WOULD I WERE WITH THEE.

PIRATE'S CHORUS.

M. W. BALFE.

MASSA'S IN THE COLD GROUND.

S. C. FOSTER.

KATY DARLING.

BELLINI.

THE HOUR FOR THEE AND ME.

R. C. FOSTER.

THE OLD PINE TREE.

C. WHITE.

ON TO THE FIELD OF GLORY.

From BELISARIO.

INTRODUCTION TO CALIPH OF BAGDAD.

ANDANTE.   BOILDIEU.

PART THIRD.

Melodies Arranged as Trios.

MARCH FROM THE DAUGHTER OF THE REGIMENT.

DONIZETTI.

WALTZ BY STRAUSS.

FOR THREE FLUTES.

BYERLY'S WALTZ.

BYERLY.

RAINBOW SCHOTTISCH.

GEMS FROM LUCIA. No. 1.

FINALE.

DONIZETTI.

GEMS FROM LUCIA. NO. 2.

Andante Cantabile.

JENNIE'S OWN SCHOTTISCH.

S. C. FOSTER.

Poco Lento.

MARIA REDOWA.

DONIZETTI.

MARIA REDOWA.---Concluded.

AIR FROM "PRECIOSA."

VON WEBER.

Allegretto grazioso.

AIR BY DE BERIOT.

PART FOURTH.

Melodies Arranged as Quartettes.

CORAL SCHOTTISCH.

H. KLEBER.

WHERE ARE THE FRIENDS OF MY YOUTH.

G. BARKER.

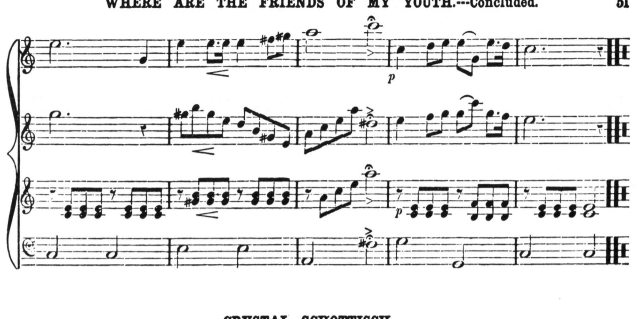

CRYSTAL SCHOTTISCH.

WM. BYERLY.

I'LL PRAY FOR THEE

DONIZETTI.

VILLAGE FESTIVAL.

QUADRILLE. No. 1.

S. C. FOSTER.

VILLAGE FESTIVAL.

VILLAGE FESTIVAL.

QUADRILLE. No. 2.

S. C. FOSTER.

VILLAGE FESTIVAL.

VILLAGE FESTIVAL.

QUADRILLE No. 3.

S. C. FOSTER.

VILLAGE FESTIVAL.

QUADRILLE No. 4.

S. C. FOSTER.

VILLAGE FESTIVAL.

JIG.

S. C. FOSTER.

No. 1. Old Folks at Home.

Arranged by S. C. FOSTER.

No. 2.—Oh, boys, carry me 'long.   S. C. FOSTER.

No. 3.—Nelly Bly.

S. C. FOSTER.

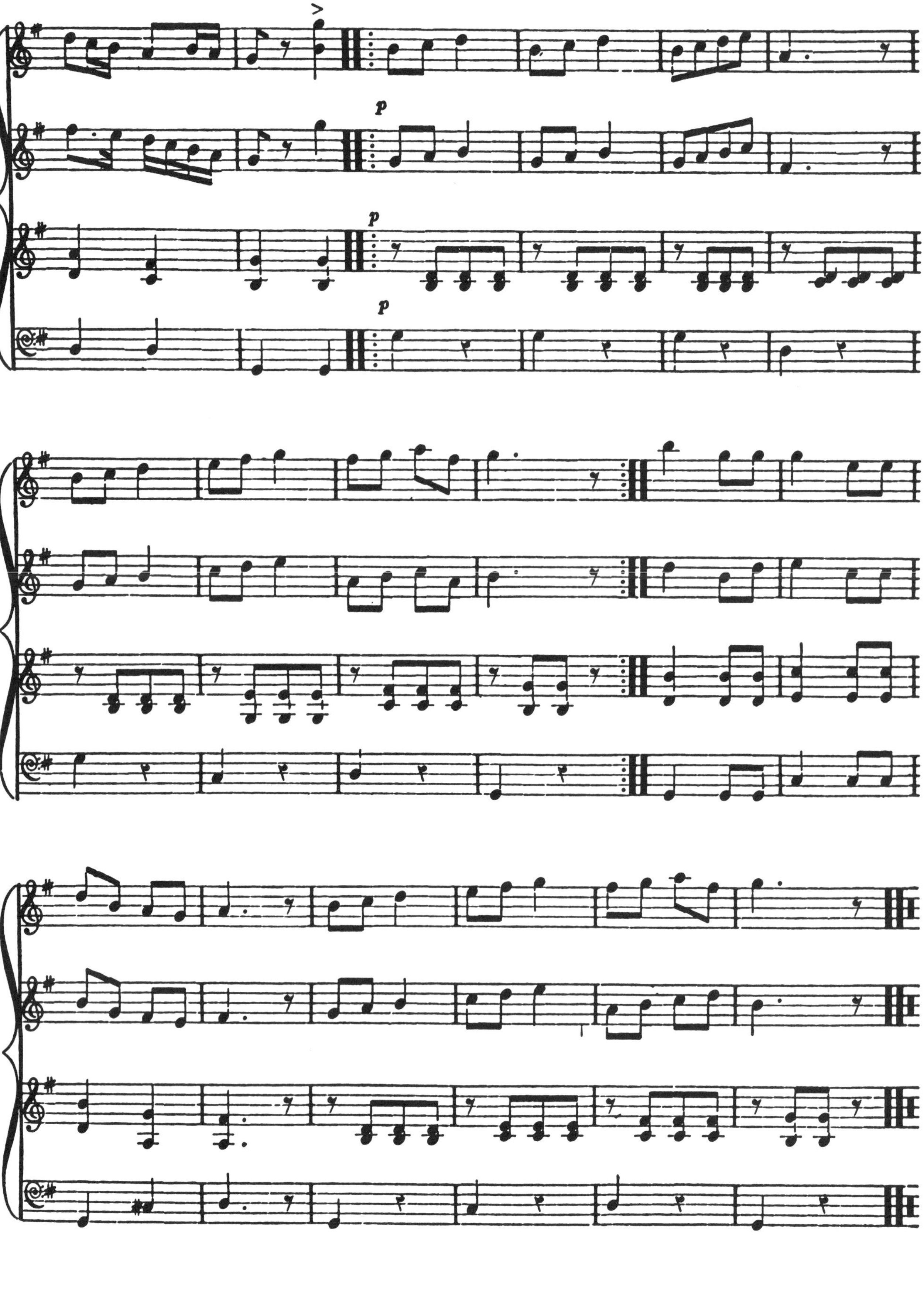
p
p
p

No. 4.—Farewell my Lilly dear.

S. C. FOSTER.

OLD FOLKS QUADRILLES. Continued.

No. 5.—Plantation Jig.

S. C. FOSTER.

FRENCH QUADRILLE.

No. 1.

TOLBEUQUE.

FRENCH QUADRILLE.

No. 2.

BOSISSIO.

FRENCH QUADRILLE---Continued.

No. 3.

BOSISSIO.

FRENCH QUADRILLE.

No. 4.   TOLBEUQUE.

1st Violin.

Flute.

2d Violin.

No. 5.

LA SÉRÉNADE.

SCHUBERT.

LA SÉRÉNADE.---Concluded.

HAPPY LAND.

E. F. RIMBAULT.